YASMIN

The Farmer

written by
SAADIA FARUQI

illustrated by
HATEM ALY

PICTURE WINDOW BOOKS
a capstone imprint

To Mariam for inspiring me, and Mubashir
for helping me find the right words—S.F.

To my sister, Eman, and her amazing girls,
Jana and Kenzi—H.A.

Yasmin is published by Picture Window Books, an imprint of Capstone.
1710 Roe Crest Drive
North Mankato, Minnesota 56003
capstonepub.com

Text copyright © 2023 by Saadia Faruqi.
Illustrations copyright © 2023 by Capstone.

Library of Congress Cataloging-in-Publication Data
Names: Faruqi, Saadia, author. | Aly, Hatem, illustrator. | Faruqi, Saadia.
Yasmin. Title: Yasmin the farmer / written by Saadia Faruqi ; illustrated
by Hatem Aly.
Description: North Mankato, Minnesota: Picture Window Books, [2022].
| Series: Yasmin | Audience: Ages 5-8. | Audience: Grades K-1. | Summary:
On her family's visit to a farm, Yasmin is thrilled to play with the baby
chicks, but when she forgets to close the pen door and one goes missing,
Yasmin has to scramble to find it.
Identifiers: LCCN 2021970059 (print) | LCCN 2021970060 (ebook) |
ISBN 9781663959317 (hardcover) | ISBN 9781666331400 (paperback) |
ISBN 9781666331417 (pdf)
Subjects: LCSH: Muslim girls—Juvenile fiction. | Pakistani Americans—
Juvenile fiction. | Chicks—Juvenile fiction. | Farms—Juvenile fiction. |
Responsibility—Juvenile fiction. | CYAC: Farms—Fiction. | Chickens—
Fiction. | Responsibility—Fiction. | Muslims—United States—Fiction. |
Pakistani Americans—Fiction.
Classification: LCC PZ7.1.F373 Ye 2022 (print) | LCC PZ7.1.F373 (ebook) |
DDC [E]—dc23
LC record available at https://lccn.loc.gov/2021970059
LC ebook record available at https://lccn.loc.gov/2021970060

Designer: Kay Fraser

Design Elements:
Shutterstock\LiukasArt

TABLE OF CONTENTS

CHAPTER ONE

A Visit to the Farm

Yasmin was excited. Today she was visiting a farm for the first time!

"I can't wait to see all the animals," Yasmin said to Mama and Baba. "Especially the baby chicks!"

"You're going to learn a
lot today, Yasmin," Baba said.
"Listen carefully and follow
directions."

"I will," Yasmin promised. She was going to be the best farmer ever!

The farm was huge. There was one red barn, two green tractors, and three big haystacks. And best of all, lots of animals!

Mama pointed to a sign with strawberries and apples on it. "We'll pick some fruit later," she said.

"But where are the baby chicks?" Yasmin asked.

A worker wearing a sun hat walked up to them. "The baby chicks are in their pen," he said, smiling. "I'm Farmer Tomás. Would you folks like to help with some chores?"

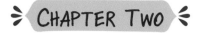

Helping Out

First, Farmer Tomás took Yasmin and her family to the stables. Yasmin rode a brown horse named Buttercup.

After her ride, Farmer Tomás showed Yasmin how to brush Buttercup's coat until it was smooth and glossy.

Then, they went to see the
sheep. Farmer Tomás showed
Yasmin how to fill their troughs
with feed. The sheep nudged
Yasmin's legs. It tickled!

Finally, they reached the

chicken coop. There were lots

of mama hens and one baba

rooster. Near the coop was a pen.

"Look, baby chicks!" Yasmin

squealed. "Can I play with

them?"

"Of course," Farmer Tomás said. "While you do that, we'll collect the eggs. Please keep the door to the pen closed."

Yasmin nodded. She went into the pen as the others headed to gather eggs. The chicks were even cuter up close!

Yasmin counted the chicks. One, two . . . seven baby chicks!

They pecked at the straw, looking for worms. They climbed over one another. One climbed onto the water dish! Yasmin giggled.

"Be good, chicks!" she said.

Cheep cheep! they replied.

Yasmin sat carefully on the ground. Looking after baby chicks was hard work.

She counted them again. One, two . . .

Uh-oh! Now there were only six chicks in the pen. Where was the seventh one?

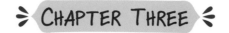

Chick in Trouble

Yasmin searched everywhere. She looked under the straw. She looked in the water dish. She looked behind big bags of seeds. No baby chick!

Then Yasmin saw that the door to the pen was open.

What would Farmer Tomás say? He'd trusted Yasmin to take care of the chicks. What would the mama hens and baba rooster think? She'd lost one of their babies!

Yasmin took a deep breath.
Farmers didn't cry. She searched
outside the pen. She looked
under a wheelbarrow. She peeked
inside a pail.

Then she heard a tiny sound.

Cheep cheep!

The missing chick! There
it was, hiding under a bush.
Yasmin picked it up and held
it close.

Farmer Tomás came over with Mama and Baba. "What happened?" he asked.

"I'm sorry I forgot to close the door," Yasmin whispered.

Farmer Tomás smiled. "We all make mistakes, Yasmin," he said. "The important thing is that you found the chick, like a good farmer."

Baba hugged Yasmin. "I'm proud of you, jaan."

"You must be hungry, Farmer Yasmin," Mama said. "Let's go pick some strawberries."

Think About It, Talk About It

* Yasmin helps Farmer Tomás with chores on the farm, like brushing the horse and feeding the sheep. Do you have any chores? Make a list of five ways you could help with tasks at home or school. Ask a friend what chores they do.

* How many farm animals can you name? Do you know what role they serve on a farm? For instance, chickens lay eggs, and sheep provide wool. Think of two other animals and why they are useful on farms.

* At the end of the story, Farmer Tomás tells Yasmin, "We all make mistakes." Think about a time you made a mistake. What did you do to fix it?

Learn Urdu with Yasmin!

Yasmin's family speaks both English and Urdu. Urdu is a language from Pakistan. Maybe you already know some Urdu words!

baba (BAH-bah)—father

hijab (HEE-jahb)—scarf covering the hair

jaan (jahn)—life; a sweet nickname for a loved one

kameez (kuh-MEEZ)—long tunic or shirt

kitaab (keh-TAB)—book

lassi (LAH-see)—a yogurt drink

nana (NAH-nah)—grandfather on mother's side

nani (NAH-nee)—grandmother on mother's side

salaam (sah-LAHM)—hello

shukriya (shuh-KREE-yuh)—thank you

Pakistan Fun Facts

Yasmin and her family are proud of their Pakistani culture. Yasmin loves to share facts about Pakistan!

Pakistan is on the continent of Asia, with India on one side and Afghanistan on the other.

The word Pakistan means "land of the pure" in Urdu and Persian.

Many languages are spoken in Pakistan, including Urdu, English, Saraiki, Punjabi, Pashto, Sindhi, and Balochi.

Pakistani farmers raise goats, sheep, cattle, and water buffalo.

The markhor is often considered the national animal of Pakistan. A markhor is a large goat with spiral shaped horns and a fur coat.

Farm Animal Match

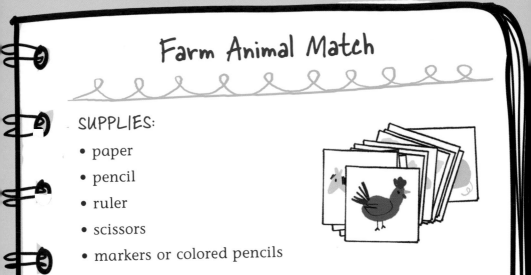

SUPPLIES:

- paper
- pencil
- ruler
- scissors
- markers or colored pencils

STEPS:

1. Cut out 12 squares of paper that are 3 x 3 inches each.

2. On each piece of paper, draw a picture of one of the following animals or baby animals: horse, foal, goat, kid, chicken, chick, pig, piglet, cow, calf, sheep, lamb. (If you're not sure what any of these animals look like, ask an adult to help you find pictures online.)

3. Find a friend and play a memory matching game! Mix up the cards, then arrange them facedown in a grid pattern. Take turns drawing two cards each. If you get a matching parent and baby animal, you keep the cards! If you don't, place the cards facedown again where you found them—and remember what they were! Then the next player takes a turn. The player with the most matches at the end wins!

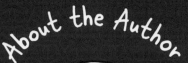

Saadia Faruqi is a Pakistani American writer, interfaith activist, and cultural sensitivity trainer featured in *O, The Oprah Magazine*. She also writes middle grade novels, such as *Yusuf Azeem Is Not A Hero*, and other books for children. Saadia is editor-in-chief of *Blue Minaret*, an online magazine of poetry, short stories, and art. Besides writing books, she also loves reading, binge-watching her favorite shows, and taking naps. She lives in Houston, Texas, with her family.

Hatem Aly is an Egyptian-born illustrator whose work has been featured in multiple publications worldwide. He currently lives in beautiful New Brunswick, Canada, with his wife, son, and more pets than people. When he is not dipping cookies in a cup of tea or staring at blank pieces of paper, he is usually drawing books. One of the books he illustrated is *The Inquisitor's Tale* by Adam Gidwitz, which won a Newbery Honor and other awards, despite Hatem's drawings of a farting dragon, a two-headed cat, and stinky cheese.

Join Yasmin on all her adventures!

   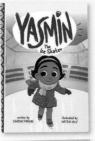

 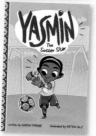